A whale putting on swimming trunks?

Is that funny?

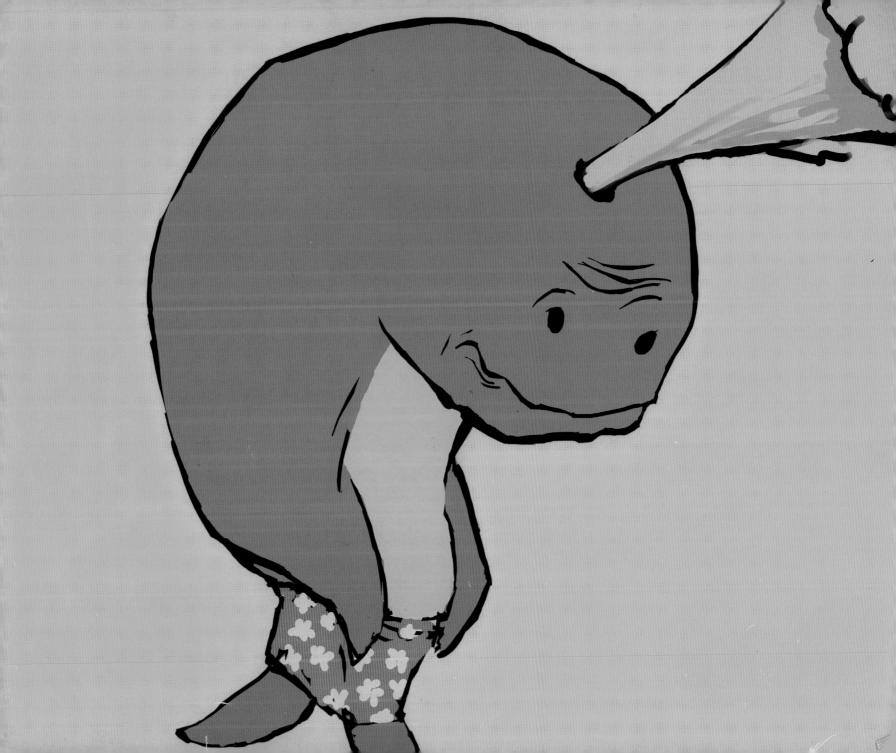

An elephant in a hot air balloon?

Is that funny?

A penguin stuck in a dartboard?

Is that funny?

Is that funny?

A starfish
in love
with
a log?

A crocodile in
an igloo?

Is that
funny?

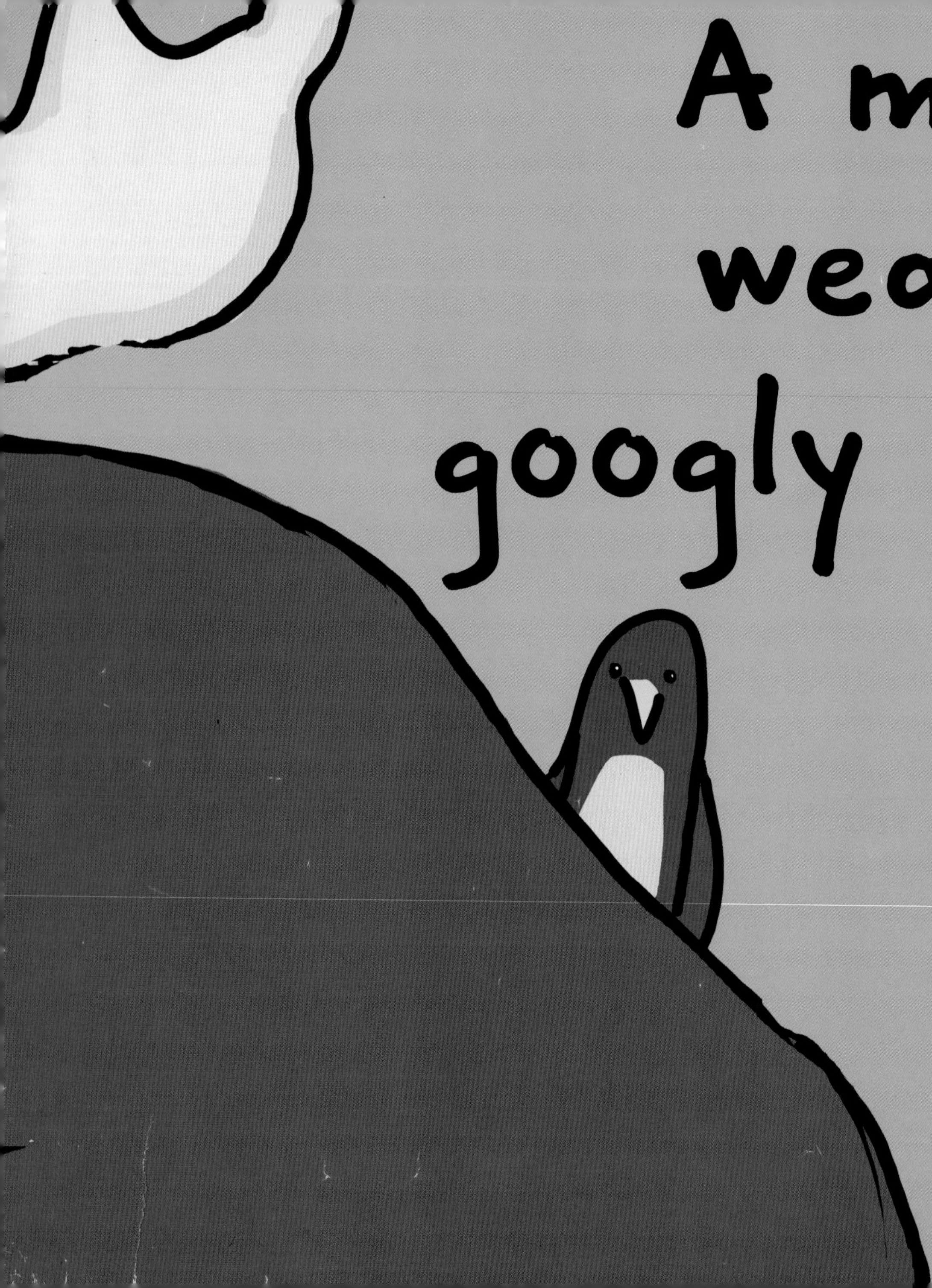

A moose wearing googly goggles?

Is that funny?

A hamster on a skateboard?

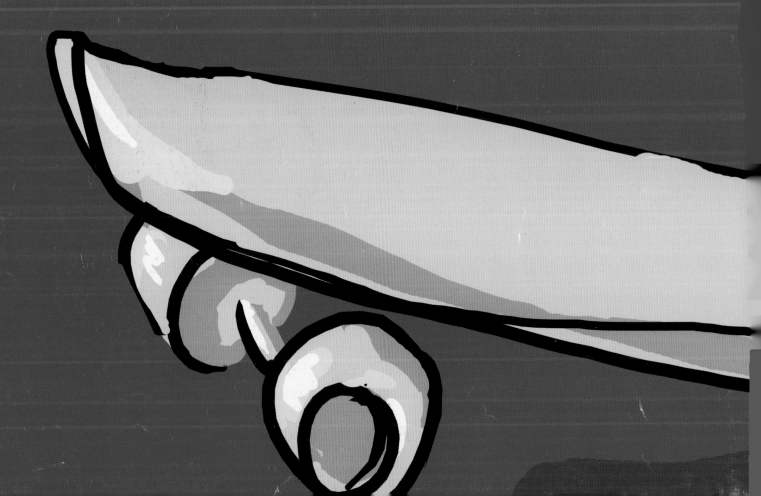

A rhino trying to eat a melon stuck on its horn?

Is that funny?

A polar bear at a song contest?

Is that funny?

A tortoise with

a hat on its back?

Is that funny?

IS THAT FUNNY?

ISBN: 0-9741319-6-2

First Edition 2006
Printed in Singapore by Tien Wah Press

CD recorded in Seoul, Korea

Distribution by Consortium Book Sales & Distribution, 1045 Westgate Drive, Suite 90, Saint Paul, MN 55114-1065, www.cbsd.com

Visit www.4npublishing.com for more information on our books.

A girl with a milk mustache?

Is THAT funny?